ZEPHIE'S
ZOOMAROUND

Bath · New York · Singapore · Hong Kong · Cologne · Delhi · Melbourne

One morning, Brewster and Zephie were going to the farm. A new lamb needed some special feed.

"Yipeeeeee!" Zephie yelled, jumping up and spinning round with excitement.

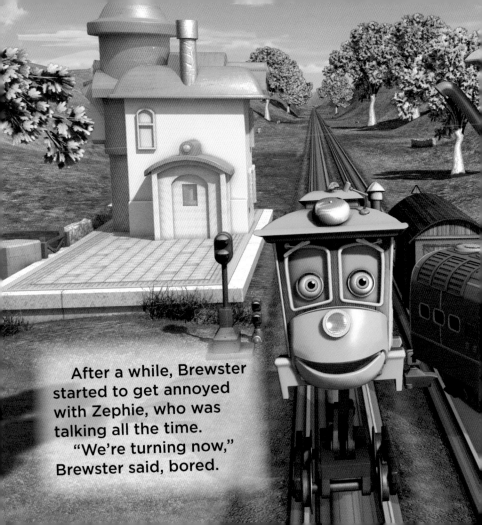

After a while, Brewster started to get annoyed with Zephie, who was talking all the time.

"We're turning now," Brewster said, bored.

Zephie didn't like being alone and started to get worried. She rang her bell, but it was too quiet for anyone to hear.

Then Olwin chugged up the track. "I was looking for the new lamb, but I got lost," Zephie told her, feeling very sorry for herself.

Olwin took Zephie to the repair shed, where Morgan fixed her with a siren. When she turned it on, it flashed and made a loud noise.

Outside the repair shed, Zephie found it fun to keep trying out her siren. Brewster and Morgan came to check on her, worried by the loud noise.

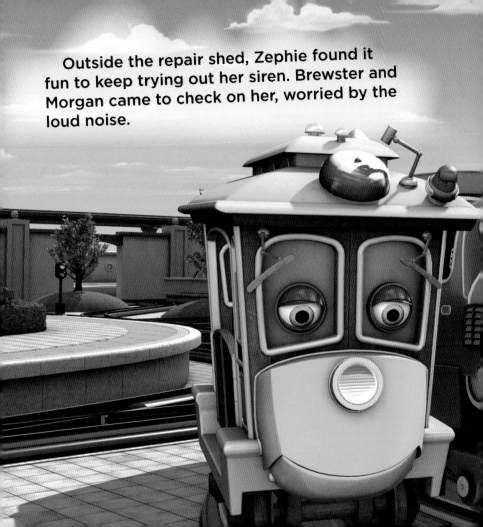

"Make sure it's an emergency next time Zephie," Eddie laughed when he realised she was just playing.

Zephie zoomed around Chuggington, searching for an emergency. At the recycling yard, Zephie thought she heard a growling noise. Then she saw some danger signs!

Scared that a lion had escaped from the safari park, she quickly set her siren off.

Dunbar sped into the recycling yard to see what the emergency was. Suddenly the growling noise stopped and Irving emerged from behind a wall.

The noise had been Irving snoring!
"You mustn't let your imagination
ride away with you," Dunbar said
sternly.

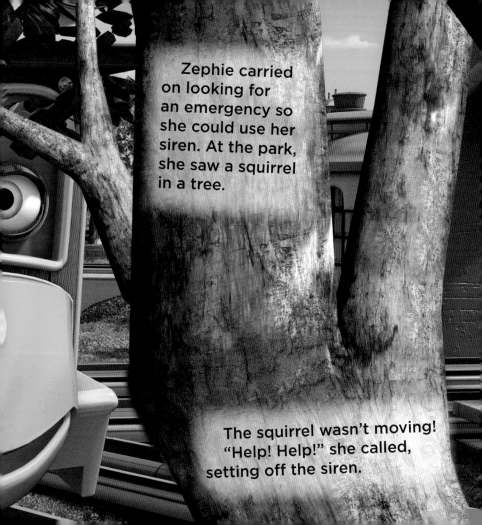

Zephie carried on looking for an emergency so she could use her siren. At the park, she saw a squirrel in a tree.

The squirrel wasn't moving! "Help! Help!" she called, setting off the siren.

Eddie rushed over and told
her that the squirrel lived in the
tree. It wasn't stuck at all!

"I don't think you're quite
ready for a siren yet Zephie,"
he said, taking it away.

"BAA!

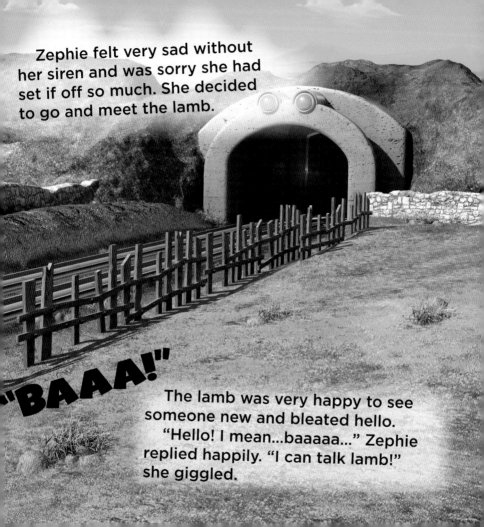

Zephie felt very sad without her siren and was sorry she had set if off so much. She decided to go and meet the lamb.

"BAAA!"

The lamb was very happy to see someone new and bleated hello.
"Hello! I mean...baaaaa..." Zephie replied happily. "I can talk lamb!" she giggled.

Zephie was so excited about the lamb she jumped up and spun around. But then she fell over and couldn't get up! Zephie tried and tried, but she was stuck.

"RESCUE CHUGGER COMING THROUGH!"

"If only I had my siren!" she yelped. Felix the farmer found Zephie and quickly telephoned for Calley to come and help.

Calley was able to get Zephie ready to ride the rails again, and brought the little chugger back to the repair shed.

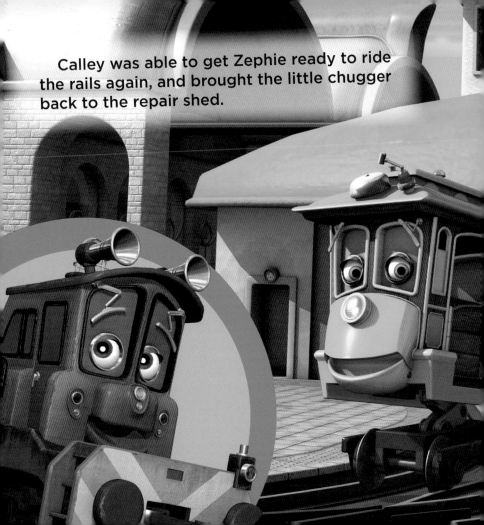

Morgan gave her siren back. "I promise, I'll only use it for real emergencies from now on!" Zephie giggled.

Can you spot five differences between these two pictures from the story?

Tick a box when you spot each difference!

1 2 3 4 5

Which track takes Morgan to Zephie?

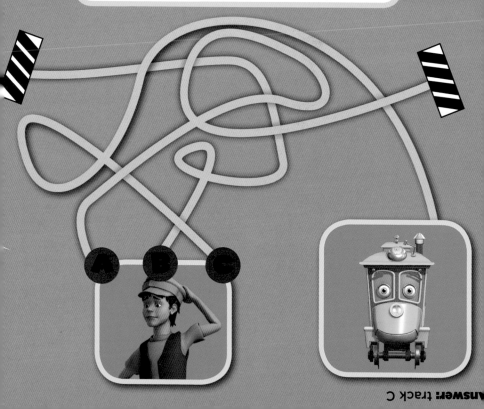

Can you draw a line to connect each sound to the correct farm animal below?

1) Moo 2) Baa 3) Tweet

Can you see which pictures of Zephie match to make a pair?

Make your own Zephie!

1. Ask an adult to help you cut out the template carefully with safety scissors.

2. Fold the tabs inwards along the dotted lines.

3. Secure tabs with glue or sticky tape.

4. Add your stickers to each side.

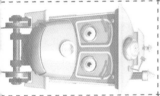

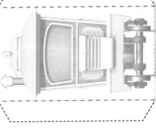

Complete your Chuggington collection.
Tick them off as you collect!

More chuggtastic books to collect!

Stories

ISBN 978-1-4075-6041-0
ISBN 978-1-4075-6042-7
ISBN 978-1-4075-6005-8
ISBN 978-1-4075-6001-4
ISBN 978-1-4075-9530-6
ISBN 978-1-4075-9531-3

Mini stories

ISBN 978-1-4075-9331-9
ISBN 978-1-4075-9332-6
ISBN 978-1-4075-9333-3
ISBN 978-1-4075-9334-0
ISBN 978-1-4075-9335-7
ISBN 978-1-4075-9336-4

Activity books

ISBN 978-1-4075-6126-4
ISBN 978-1-4075-6044-1
ISBN 978-1-4075-6145-5
ISBN 978-1-4075-9529-0
ISBN 978-1-4075-9422-4
Little library ISBN 978-1-4075-6043-4

Multi-play books

ISBN 978-1-4075-9882-6
ISBN 978-1-4075-9884-0
Annual ISBN 978-1-84535-437-4
Activity pack
ISBN 978-1-4075-9885-7
3D books ISBN 978-1-4075-8349-5
ISBN 978-1-4075-9780-5

Play books

ISBN 978-1-4075-6127-1
ISBN 978-1-4075-8142-2
Story collection ISBN 978-1-4075-6046-5
Train books
ISBN 978-1-4075-8138-5
ISBN 978-1-4075-8139-2
ISBN 978-1-4075-8140-8